"The Rambunctious Tommy Turnpike"

created and written
by
a.t.johnson

illustrated
by
seijin ishida

Tommy Turnpike was born
Thomas P. Turnpike in BeeBop
City, U.S.A. The doctor and
nurses marveled what a darling
little tyke he was!

His parents, Tina and Thomas
Sr. were proud of their little
Tommy. He was a happy little
baby who cooed and laughed a lot.

Tommy, however, was a very curious
little boy. He couldn't sit still.
Tommy liked to wander.

When Tommy was 1, he wanted some fun. He removed his red bib, climbed out of his crib and you'll never believe what he did.

4

He took a stroll around town,
passed jugglers and clowns and
saw a puppy dog wearing a frown.

He passed the Baker, a Quaker,
a Hat and Shoemaker.

He climbed Sky Scraping
Cranes and looked at Big Planes.

7

He hitched a ride on a train and
started to sing with Hobos
and Dough Boys and some
he did not know.

He walked to the park where he
sang with a lark and strolled down
the lane with Old Man Clark.

But back at his home, Tommy's parents were frantic! Their Tommy was missing and oh how they panicked!

10

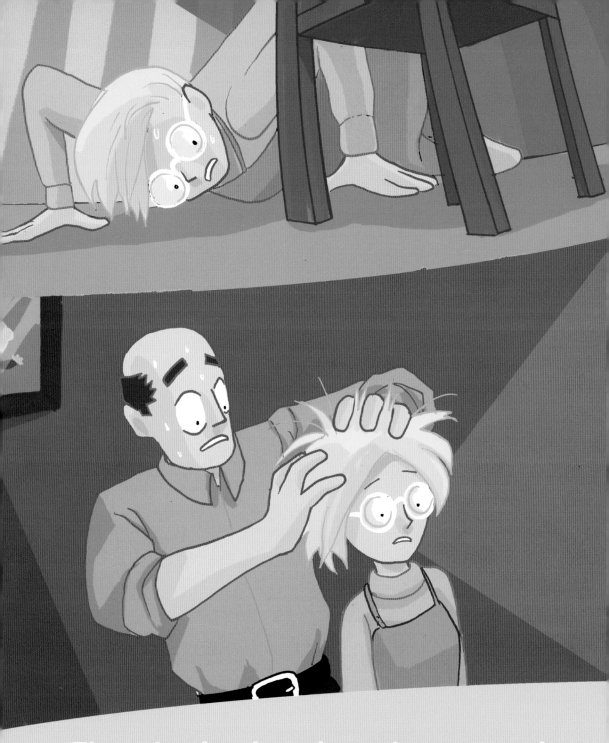

They looked under chairs, and
they looked in their hair.

They went to the fair where they asked the gray mare...but Tommy could not be found.

12

They hopped on a stork who flew as far as New York...but Tommy could not be found!

The sun had gone down. They were wearing big frowns. But still...Tommy had not been found.

At a quarter to four, there was a knock on the door and Tommy was lost no more!

His parents, they sighed, they looked in his eyes but Tommy would only say, "hi".

"Where have you been?" they
asked again and again. But
Tommy just said, "with friends".

"I went to the park where I sang
with a lark and chatted with
old man Clark."

"You went to the park!" "You sang with a lark!" "We were worried, you know, it was dark!"

20

Tommy felt sad. He kissed his mom and dad and said he would be a good lad.

They put him to bed. They both kissed his head and little Tommy soon fell asleep.

coordinator/editor leigh ann whetstone

visit tommy at:
tommyturnpike.com

ISBN 0-9773760-0-1

Printed in Hong Kong by Regal Printing